Samuel French Acting Edition

Jack and the Soy Beanstalk

Book and Lyrics by
Jerrod Bogard

Music by
Sky Seals and Emily Fellner

FOR PRODUCTION INQUIRIES

UNITED STATES AND CANADA
info@concordtheatricals.com
1-866-979-0447

UNITED KINGDOM AND EUROPE
licensing@concordtheatricals.co.uk
020-7054-7200

Each title is subject to availability from Concord Theatricals Corp., depending upon country of performance. Please be aware that *JACK AND THE SOY BEANSTALK* may not be licensed by Concord Theatricals Corp. in your territory. Professional and amateur producers should contact the nearest Concord Theatricals Corp. office or licensing partner to verify availability.

No one shall make any changes in this title(s) for the purpose of production. No part of this book may be reproduced, stored in a retrieval system, scanned, uploaded, or transmitted in any form, by any means, now known or yet to be invented, including mechanical, electronic, digital, photocopying, recording, videotaping, or otherwise, without the prior written permission of the publisher. No one shall share this title(s), or any part of this title(s), through any social media or file hosting websites.

For all inquiries regarding motion picture, television, online/digital and other media rights, please contact Concord Theatricals Corp.

MUSIC AND THIRD PARTY MATERIALS USE NOTE

Licensees are solely responsible for obtaining formal written permission from copyright owners to use copyrighted music and/or other copyrighted third-party materials (e.g., artworks, logos) in the performance of this play and are strongly cautioned to do so. If no such permission is obtained by the licensee, then the licensee must use only original music and materials that the licensee owns and controls. Licensees are solely responsible and liable for clearances of all third-party copyrighted materials, including without limitation music, and shall indemnify the copyright owners of the play(s) and their licensing agent, Concord Theatricals Corp., against any costs, expenses, losses and liabilities arising from the use of such copyrighted third-party materials by licensees. For music, please contact the appropriate music licensing authority in your territory for the rights to any incidental music.

IMPORTANT BILLING AND CREDIT REQUIREMENTS

If you have obtained performance rights to this title, please refer to your licensing agreement for important billing and credit requirements.

JACK AND THE SOY BEANSTALK was commissioned by Wide Eyed Productions, under the artistic direction of Kristin Skye Hoffmann, in the fall of 2008. It premiered in New York City at the New York International Fringe Festival (a presentation of The Present Company) on August 15, 2009. It was directed by Jerrod Bogard, with music direction by Sky Seals, arrangements by Emily Fellner, choreography by Nam Holtz, set & puppet design by Jerrod Bogard, scenic art by Jen McDuffee, and lighting design by Ryan Metzler. The production stage managers were Matt Bresler and Megan Jupin. The cast was as follows:

JACK. . . . . Carlos Avilas*

MOMMA . . . . .Laura Hall*

MRS. BIG . . . . Brianne Mai

SECURITY GUARD, MR. BIG . . . . Okieriete Onaodowan

THE i-HARP . . . . .Jake Paque

THE MINSTREL . . . . Sky Seals*

JACK (SWING) . . . . Sage Seals

*Appeared courtesy of Actors' Equity Association

CHARACTER DESCRIPTIONS

MINSTREL – The helpful, guitar playing story-teller and friend to all.

JACK – An all-American boy. Still young enough to get sent to bed without any supper. He's curious, adventurous, inventive, and he loves his video games.

MOMMA – A working mom. She loves her boy, Jack, and believes she can make a difference in the world by doing her part.

SECURITY GUARD – A gruff task-master working for the big industrial farm.

FARMER – The wacky farmer running Magic Acre Farms.

MRS. BIG – The Giant's wife. A ruthless woman who cares about nothing but herself and her money.

GOLDEN i-HARP – A singing, rapping, golden mp3 player, and Mr. Big's henchman.

MR. BIG – The Giant President of Big Aggie Reaping Farms Inc. He's so big, you may only be able to see his feet. He only cares about the bottom line.

GOLDEN GOOSE – The goose that lays the golden eggs. Probably played by a stuffed puppet goose. Only says one word: HONK!!!

(Please note: there may be character doubling. The actor playing the Security guard may double as Mr. Big, The Minstrel may double as the Farmer, and Momma may double as Mrs. Big.)

THE SET

The stage is bare except for a Shadow Puppet Screen. This screen can be used to hang drops on or attach scenery to as the play moves forward. The screen can also act as a place of entrance and exit for the actors.

Periodically the screen will be lighted from behind and used to tell Shadow Puppet Stories using very simple, cardboard shadow puppets.

There are many books and websites that will teach you to make beautiful, inexpensive shadow puppets, and creating them can be a super fun project. Of course, shadow puppetry is not the only way to tell this story, and the segments described here merely represent how the author designed and directed the original production.

MUSICAL NUMBERS

SCENE ONE:

1. *You Don't Know Jack* (**ENTIRE CAST**)

SCENE THREE:

2. *Wind Power* (**JACK, MINSTREL**)

SCENE FOUR:

3. *Blown Around* (**JACK**)

4. *The Magic Bean* (**JACK, FARMER, BEAN-PODS**)

SCENE FIVE:

5. *Momma's Song* (**MOMMA**)

SCENE SIX:

6. *Things You Throw Away* (**MINSTREL**)

SCENE SEVEN:

7. *Fingers To The Bone* (**MRS. BIG, JACK**)

SCENE EIGHT:

8. *The Golden Goose* (**MR. BIG, GOLDEN I-HARP, MINSTREL**)

9. *The Chase* (Instrumental)

SCENE NINE:

10. *Momma's Song 2* (**MOMMA**)

11. *The Chase 2;* (Instrumental)

12. *Finale:*

You Don't Know Jack – reprise; (**MINSTREL**)

Things You Throw Away – reprise; (**ENTIRE CAST**)

Scene One: Introductions

(The **MINSTREL** *enters. He's searching for his fellow storytellers and calling their names. Embarrassed that he's all alone, he turns to the audience.)*

MINSTREL. Hi. Hello. My name is *(name of actor)*. I get to play the Minstrel in today's play. Do you know what a minstrel is?…A minstrel is a person who travels around playing music and telling stories with his songs. Oh yeah! And you know what? With this guitar I can tell you stories without even using words. Here, I'll show you what I mean. When I play a chord on my guitar like this – *(plays a major chord)* – Does that sound happy or sad to you? Kind of happy, right?! And how about when I play a chord like this – *(plays a minor chord)* – What's that sound like?…Kind of sad, yeah. Wait-wait-wait – What's this sound like? – *(plays a dominant chord)* What's that?…Kind of confusing, yeah. Today when we sing songs, you'll get part of the story through the words, and you'll get part of the story through the music. Well, that is if I can find the other actors…Wait. I have an idea. Maybe if I sing a song, then they'll hear me and come running.

(singing and playing)

WHERE ARE THE ACTORS?
WHERE ARE THE ACTORS?

(The other actors rush onto the stage from all directions. They strike a pose and sing:)

ALL.

WE'RE RIGHT HERE!!!

MINSTREL. Alright! Yeah! Now, if you'll give us just a second, we've got to decide which story we're going to tell you today.

(The actors huddle and discuss in private.)

ACTOR #1. Catcher in the Rye!

(beat)

MINSTREL. Today we'll be telling the story of Jack and the Beanstalk!

*(The actors all rush backstage to prepare, but **ACTOR #1** lingers behind with the **MINSTREL**.)*

ACTOR #1. 'Scuse me, sorry, uhm… I know we're supposed to be telling the story of Jack and the Beanstalk, but uhm, see, I just don't understand why Jack would do what he did in the story.

MINSTREL. Well, *(name of **ACTOR #1**)*, let me ask you a question…

SONG: YOU DON'T KNOW JACK

MINSTREL.

WOULD YOU TRADE ALL YOUR ALLOWANCE FOR
A POCKET FULL OF BEANS?
DID YOU EVER KNOW SOMEBODY WHO'D DO THAT?
IF YOU'VE NEVER MET A PERSON WHO COULD
BE JUST THAT NAÏVE,
THEN I CAN TELL THAT YOU JUST DON'T KNOW JACK.

We all know how he traded his family cow for a pocket full of…a pocket full of…uh-oh I've forgotten. A pocket full of what?

ACTOR #1. Lollipops! *(may adlib item)*

ACTOR #2. Pencil shavings! *(may adlib item)*

ACTOR #3. It was a pocket full of Scrabble letters! *(may adlib item)*

MINSTREL. No, that's not it. What was it?… ["Beans!"]… Beans? Just ordinary old beans? No?… ["Magic Beans!"] …Magic beans?! Traded his family cow for a pocket full of magic beans? What a moron! But then, you know what? Something magnificent came out of that crazy decision, didn't it?

SAY, HAVE YOU EVER FOLLOWED
A TRAIL INTO THE WOODS
NOT SURE YOU'D EVER FIND THE RIGHT WAY BACK?
WELL, IF YOU SAY WOULDN'T,
UNLESS YOU KNEW YOU COULD
I'M TELLING YOU THAT YOU JUST DON'T KNOW JACK.

(The **CAST** *have gone backstage and now they enter in a group. They're pushing onstage the curious, but somewhat reluctant little boy,* **JACK***.)*

I wish Jack were here right now. Right here in this theater *(or library, school cafeteria etc.)* I'd love to hear this story from Jack himself. Wouldn't you?

(The group pushes **JACK** *forward.)*

JACK. Hi… I'm Jack.

MINSTREL. Well, HI, JACK!
IT'S NICE TO MEET YOU.

JACK.
NICE TO MEET YOU.

MINSTREL. Sit down and take a load off. DROP YOUR PACK.

JACK. Thanks a bunch!

MINSTREL.
WE'D LIKE TO HEAR THE STORY
OF YOUR BEANSTALK CLIMBING GLORY

JACK.
DON'T ALL OF YOU ALREADY KNOW ALL THAT?

(Music slows and softens.)

Well, uhm.
SURE WE'VE HEARD THE RUMORS
YES, SURE WE'VE HEARD THE TALES
BUT WE'D LIKE TO MAKE REAL SURE WE KNOW THE FACTS.
SO IF YOU'VE GOT A FEW
WE'D LIKE TO HEAR IT ALL FROM YOU
WE'D REALLY LIKE TO KNOW THAT WE KNOW JACK.

JACK. I'll tell you of my tale, every last detail,

It's funny, touching, and it's action packed.

And when the telling's through,

I'll be a friend to each of you,

and you will also be a friend to me… I'm Jack.

(Music picks up volume and speed.)

MINSTREL.

HI JACK!

IT'S NICE TO MEET YOU.

JACK.

NICE TO MEET YOU.

MINSTREL.

SIT DOWN AND TAKE A LOAD OFF. DROP YOUR PACK.

JACK. That's very nice.

MINSTREL.

WE'D LIKE TO HEAR THE STORY

OF YOUR GIANT KILLING GLORY

JACK. I'm sorry. Wait.

(Music stops.)

First of all – there's no glory in killing. None at all. And I'm very sorry for what happened to that poor giant.

(Music comes back in softly.)

MINSTREL. "Poor" giant? But I thought he was rich-rich-rich.

JACK. Yeah, of course, he had more money than Batman, but he was a sad and lonely giant, and so though he was rich in money, he was very poor in spirit. But we're starting at the wrong place. We should begin this story from the very tippy-top. From the start I mean. And this story begins in the same way that all of the most important stories do… Once Upon A Time…

MINSTREL.

ONCE UPON A TIME

JACK. Yes, Once Upon A Time.

MINSTREL.

YOU TELL THE TALE

JACK.

AND YOU KEEP US ON TRACK.

MINSTREL. It's a deal!

AND WE ALL WILL PRETEND
WITH YOU UNTIL "THE END"
SO NO ONE SAYS THAT WE DON'T KNOW
THE STORY FRONT TO BACK

NO, NO ONE'S GONNA SAY ———
WE DON'T KNOW JACK.

Well, they won't.

Scene Two: Chores

JACK. Once upon a time…about an hour after school. Upon that time specifically I mean – Momma came into the living room and interrupted me while I was doing my chores.

(**JACK** *grabs his video game controller and sits on the floor facing the shadow screen.*

(Shadow Puppet Show: [A classic video game.] A little man bounces his way through an obstacle course of tubes and blocks. When he hits a block with his head, a little beanstalk grows out of the big tube.)

(NOTE: The actors behind the screen make the sounds and music of the video game and all the other shadow puppet sequences.)

MOMMA. Jack! Jack, get off that X-Station Playbox right now and –

JACK. But Momma, I'm about to conquer this world. You want me to conquer the world don't you?

*(***MOMMA*** enters.)*

MOMMA. Jackaroo Sproutmire Beanpole.

MINSTREL. "Jackaroo?" Ouch.

MOMMA. If I have told you once, I've told you a thousand times: it is high time you started pulling your weight around here; money doesn't grow on trees; life isn't fair; the world doesn't revolve around Jack; I'm not your maid, I'm not made of money, and I'm not joking mister; it's all fun and games until somebody loses an eye, as long as you live under my roof you'll live by my rules, and,… Hm. Am I forgetting anything? Ah-yes.

JACK. But why –

MOMMA. Because I said so!

JACK. Awww Momma!

MOMMA. Now I want you to get off your lazy, daydreaming keester and go run me an errand.

JACK. Walk the dog?

MOMMA. We sold the dog.

JACK. Walk the cat?

MOMMA. We sold the cat.

JACK. Walk the plank?

MOMMA. We never had a plank, but if we did –

JACK. We'd have sold it?

MOMMA. You got that right. We're poor Jack. Poor poor poor. Which is why we have to sell the family pick-up truck. Now – you must take the pick-up truck and try to sell it to one of the farmers who live just outside of town.

JACK. Sell Old Smoky? But why? Can't we just sell my little brother instead?

MOMMA. We sold him two weeks ago. It was either him or your video games.

JACK. Good choice.

MOMMA. And now we have to sell the pick-up truck, because gasoline is one hundred ga-billion dollars a gallon, Jack. We just can't afford to keep it. We can't afford to drive it. We can't even afford to drive it to the place you're going to sell it. You'll have to push it all the way.

JACK. What!?

MOMMA. I siphoned all the gas out of the tank and I'm going to use this *(holds up a gas can)* to pay for a new, hybrid-electric-solar car that runs on the power of the sun, the sound of its own horn, and the most powerful resource of all, good old American willpower.

JACK. I don't think a car like that exists, Momma.

MOMMA. Well not with that attitude it doesn't. Go, take Ol' Smokey and make sure you get a fair price for her. Those farmers can be tricky. One time I went out to the farms to get some vegetables for a dinner party I was planning. I purchased a bag full of tomatoes, but when I got home I realized that he'd given me a bag full of tomatoes *(pronounced "to-mau-toes")*.

JACK. What did you do?

MOMMA. I called the whole thing off. Go now, go, but – make sure you are back before the streetlights come on. Stay on the main highway and then come straight home.

(She kisses him goodbye and exits. He wipes his face.)

MINSTREL. *(to audience)* Not being able to drive the pick-up made Jack's task a far more difficult one. Not only was it quite a far journey, it was also a very hot day.

JACK. I'd better empty the bed of the truck. If it's lighter it'll be easier to push.

MINSTREL. Jack decided to empty the bed of the truck so it would be easier to push.

JACK. Let's see what we've got back here. Camping gear? Hey yeah! It's dad's old camping tent! His old fishing pole. And here's his trusty axe.

MINSTREL. The sun was blazing overhead. Jack wiped his brow and thought,

JACK.	MINSTREL.
At least there's a nice breeze blowing.	At least there's a nice breeze blowing – breeze blowing – breeze blowing.

JACK. A breeze eh?… Hmm.

MINSTREL. Just then…

JACK. Gives me an idea.

MINSTREL. Jack got an idea, and he went right to work.

(JACK steps behind the shadow screen – we see shadows and hear sounds of construction.)

MINSTREL. Jack knew what he wanted. He wanted that truck to move without having to push it. But he only had certain things he could use to make that happen.

(With the first two shadows revealed the actors backstage make "Ta-dah!" sounds. On the last one, the axe, the actors make the famous string sounds from the murder scene in the film "Psycho.")

JACK. The tent! *(a tent shaped shadow)* The Fishing Pole! *(fishing pole shadow)* The axe! *(an axe shadow).*

MINSTREL. Each step seemed to lead to another five even harder steps, but Jack just kept working until he had an entirely new creation. Proving – of course – that imagination is a renewable resource.

ACTOR #1. Introducing!…The world's first wind powered pick-up truck. Ol' Windy!

(**JACK** *produces a pick-up truck with a wind sail sticking out of the roof. The sail is made from the fishing pole and the tent.)*

MINSTREL. Wowee. How did you think this up, Jack?

JACK. I guess it just made good sense.

MINSTREL. Well alright! But do you know if it's going to work?

JACK. No idea really. But as long as the wind keeps blowing then the wheels should keep rolling, don't you think?

MINSTREL. But Jack –

JACK. Sorry! Got ground to cover! The wind is picking up!

MINSTREL. But how will you know which way the wind is blowing?! Jack!!!

(**JACK** *"drives away." Lights out.)*

Scene Three: Traveling

(Lights up on the highway. **JACK** *is riding the wind-truck, steering it with the sail.)*

SONG: WIND POWER

JACK. Holy cow, I'm really truckin' here.
THE WIND IS PUSHIN ME FORWARD
PUSHIN ME TOWARD
SOMETHING THAT I'VE GOT TO DO

THIS POWER GIVING ME MOTION
GIVES ME THE NOTION
THAT IT'S GONNA SEE ME THROUGH

CUZ IT'S A BREEZE TO SEE
THE INVISIBLE SOURCE OF THIS COURSE I'M RIDING
IT'S THE BREEZE THAT WE
CAN'T SEE, BUT WE FEEL, AND IT'S SO EXCITING

*(The scenery changes from urban to suburban to bucolic
– green fields and windmills.)*

Wow. It's so beautiful out here. No billboards blocking
the scenery. Everything's so green.
CUZ IT'S A BREEZE TO SEE
THE INVISIBLE SOURCE OF THIS COURSE I'M RIDING
IT'S THE BREEZE THAT WE
CAN'T SEE, BUT WE FEEL, AND IT'S SO EXCITING
Here we go, I see a sign up ahead. "Big Aggie Reaping
Farms, Inc." This place sounds like they mean busi-
ness, and business is what I came to do.

*(He stops the wind-truck in front of the big gate and dis-
mounts the truck. The* **SECURITY GUARD** *appears. He
has a cardboard walky-talky. He likes to speak into it
and make it squawk – "CHSHH!")*

JACK. Hi, there.

SECURITY. Evening, sir. Help you?

JACK. Hope so. My mom sent me out here to sell our truck.

SECURITY. Oh yeah?

JACK. Yeah. Interested?

SECURITY. No.

JACK. Not you though, I mean the farmer.

SECURITY. There's no farmer here. Where do you think you are?

JACK. Uhm,… a farm? It's a good truck.

SECURITY. Look in there. Go on. Have a peek through the gate there. See in there?

JACK. Yeah.

SECURITY. Yeah? Whataya see in there, huh?

JACK. There's a lot of –

SECURITY. Trucks.

JACK. And –

SECURITY. Tractors.

JACK. And –

SECURITY. And the tallest grain silos you've ever seen for as far as your eye can see. Big Aggie Reaping Farms doesn't want your truck. We're industrial! We've got trucks that bring the seed, trucks that dump the fertil-izer, trucks that harvest the crop, and trucks that then deliver it to supermarkets across the entire country. Flatbed trucks, tractor-trailer trucks, even air-condi-tioned trucks for our poultry and dairy products.

JACK. Oh. OK. But…what if one of the trucks breaks down?

SECURITY. We call the tow-truck and he trucks the broken down truck to the truck repair. *(into walky-talky)* CHSHH! Over.

JACK. Oh. Hm. Well, do you have a wind-truck?

SECURITY. Wind-truck? Why would we truck the wind? It blows from place to place on its own.

JACK. No, see, when we ran out of gas I got this idea –

SECURITY. Kid. Hey. Big Aggie Reaping Farms doesn't want your cute little truck or your cute little ideas. Now scram before I call the security truck.

JACK. Oh you –

SECURITY. We have a truck for that, yes.

JACK. OK. I'll go. Can you tell me though, is there another farm around that might want to buy my pick-up? Maybe a small farm without so many trucks?

SECURITY. A "small" farm? Hahaha! Kid, you saw those big grain silos? They are so tall and so numerous that they block the sun for miles.

JACK. But –

SECURITY. CHSHH! And miles.

JACK. But plants can't grow without sunlight.

SECURITY. Now you're catchin' on. There are no "small farms" in the shadow of an industrial farm like this. Not anymore.

(JACK climbs onto the wind-truck, puts on his helmet and unravels the sail.)

SECURITY. *(into his walky-talky)* Hey Mac, I'm starving. Send over the lunch truck, would ya? *(He goes to leave – stopping one last time.)* CHSHH! Ooover.

(He exits.)

Scene Four: Magic Acre Farms

*(Back on the road – **JACK** on his wind-truck.)*

MINSTREL. Well that was a bust. And here we thought the wind was blowing you right where you needed to be. What did you do then?

JACK. What could I do? I headed for home. But then something strange happened! The wind – it wouldn't blow the way it was supposed to! Hey wind! You're blowing the wrong way. Town is back the other – woohh!!

*(The wind-truck takes a sudden turn and races out of control. **JACK** holds on for dear life.)*

SONG: BLOWN AROUND

JACK.

THE WIND IS BLOWING ME AROUND
AND PUSHING ME AROUND
AND SPINNING ME AROUND
WHERE AM I
GOING ANY WAY THAT I AM BLOWN
GOING FAR AWAY FROM HOME
GOING TO A PLACE THAT I HAVE
NEVER KNOWN.

WHEN I SET OUT ON THIS JOURNEY
I KNEW EVERY SMALL DETAIL
NOW THE WORLD'S GETTING BLURRY
AFRAID I MIGHT HAVE TO BAIL.

OH THE WIND KEEPS BLOWING ALL AROUND
BUT I'M RIDING IT AROUND
NOW I'M NOT AFRAID TO
STAND MY GROUND
NOW I SEE MY PATH IS ALWAYS MINE
GONNA STEP UP TO THE LINE
AND I THINK I'M GONNA CRASH INTO THAT SIGN!

(Shadow Puppet Show: The wind-truck goes spinning out of control. A big sign leaps to the screen: "SPLAT!" or "CRASH!" – The actors make sound effects backstage.)

(**JACK** *falls free of his truck. Lights up. A sign nearby reads, "Magic Acre Farms."*)

JACK. *(cont.)* Ah! Ah! Ground! Sweet, delicious dirt. Muah Muah. Akk – Akk. Dirty, gross dirt. Ptooey Ptooey.

FARMER'S VOICE. *(from off stage)* What in the E. I. E. I. O. is goin' on out there!?

(Enter a **FARMER.***)*

FARMER. Well hello there, young man. You OK?

JACK. Hi. Yes, I'm fine. Sorry about your lawn.

FARMER. Oh, that's just fine. Grass grows back. Say, that's a right nice lookin' wind-truck ya got there.

JACK. Yeah? Well, it works great when the wind doesn't suddenly change and start blowing in directions you weren't expecting.

FARMER. Yes, I suppose some things are just plain unpredictable. One thing's for sure though, you don't need a weatherman to see which way the wind blows.

JACK. Maybe not, but I could use a road map to see which way this road goes. I'm one hundred percent totally lost.

FARMER. Well, how can that be? I'm here with you, and I'm not lost. We're on Magic Acre Farm.

JACK. Magic Acre Farm? This is a lot different then the last farm I saw.

FARMER. That's because this is a local farm, my boy! This is where you get food straight from the ground like good ol' Momma Nature intended.

JACK. Oh, and so you're the farmer here, huh? You said that you liked my wind-truck. Well, would you like to buy it? Because it's totally for sale.

FARMER. Hmm, "totally," you say? Well, it is a pretty special little boy who could come up with an invention like this – a little boy who's not afraid of a little, adventure. Yes…. I'll buy your truck. I will give you…seventeen.

JACK. Sell our family truck for seventeen dollars?! Are you crazy?

FARMER. Not seventeen dollars. Seventeen beans.

JACK. Sell our family truck for seventeen beans?! Do you think *I'm* crazy?

FARMER. They're not just any old beans. They're magic beans.

JACK. You want me to sell our family truck for seventeen magic beans. Well that's at least sounding a little more reasonable. But wait a second, before I make some crazy decision, tell me what makes these beans so magic.

SONG: THE MAGIC BEAN

FARMER.

> IF YOU HAVE AN ACRE
> ON WHICH YOU NEED TO GROW
> SOME FRUITS OR VEGE-TABLES
> THAT THEN YOU'D LIKE TO SOW
>
> THERE'S A PLANT THAT'S HARDY,
> TASTY, AND NUTRISH,
> THAT'S PERFECT IN MOST ANY
> CULINARY DISH.
>
> *(During the next verse – green soybean pod puppets appear from behind the screen. They're very cute – Muppet-style hand puppets. They're "looking around.")*
>
> OH IT'S SOY, SOY, SOY, SOY
> IT'S A MAGIC BEAN MY BOY
> NOTHING CAN BRING SUCH JOY
> AS THIS MAGIC BEAN CALLED SOY
>
> *(The soybean pods open their mouths and bebop to the music! And they "bebop" through most of the song…)*

BEAN PODS.

> BOP! BOP! BE-BOP SHUWAP!

FARMER.

> SOY SAUCE MAKES YOUR PLAIN OLD RICE
> DARK AND TANGY, TASTES SO NICE
> SOY MILK IN YOUR BREAKFAST BOWL
> IF YOU'RE LACTOSE INTOLERABLE

FARMER. *(cont.)*

    ICE CREAM, YOGURT, CHEESE AND CHIPS,
    A CREAMY TOPPING, LIGHTLY WHIPPED.
    HIGH IN PROTIEN MUSCLES CRAVE
    ROASTED, SALTED: EDAMAME

        CREAMER FOR YOUR COFFEE
        AND COFFEE IN YOUR CUP,
        SOY CAN MAKE MOST ANYTHING
        THAT YOU CAN THINK UP.

        AND NOT JUST THINGS THAT YOU CAN EAT
        BUT ALSO THINGS YOU CAN'T
        SOY CAN MAKE MOST ANYTHING
        CUZ IT'S A MAGIC PLANT.

    (CHORUS)

        SCIENTISTS ARE WORKING
        AND LEARNING EVERY DAY
        NEW USES FOR THIS MAGIC PLANT
        THAT BLOW MY MIND AWAY

Sing for your supper beans!

(The bean pods scat for 12 bars.)

(CHORUS)

(Song ends.)

So, whataya say? Is it a deal?

(Blackout)

Scene Five: Back at Home

*(Lights up at **JACK**'s house.)*

MOMMA.
WHERE IS MY YOUNG AND BEAMISH BOY?
MY HEART IS SICK WITH WORRY.
THE STREETLIGHTS NOW ARE COMING ON
JACK, MY SON, PLEASE HURRY.

*(enter **JACK**.)*

JACK. I made it!

MOMMA. You made it!

JACK. I sold the truck!

MOMMA. You sold the truck!

JACK. I traded it for 17 magic beans!

MOMMA. You what'd it for the what-what?

JACK. Magic beans, Momma.

MOMMA. You didn't.

MINSTREL. He sure did.

JACK. And the farmer threw in this bag of fertilizer and these attractive gardening gloves – for free! We'll grow the most magical crop you've ever seen, Momma! A great big crop of soy!

MOMMA. The only thing you're growing is a great big crop of you're grounded. I told you to get money, Jack, not useless beans! You are grounded. No dinner tonight, and absolutely no video games.

JACK. But –

MOMMA. No TV. No Internet.

JACK. But –

MOMMA. No comic books. No baseball cards. No action figures.

JACK. *(aside)* At least I'll still have my –

MOMMA. And definitely no iPod!

JACK. Doh!

MOMMA. Now I have to sell all those things just to make up the money you've lost with your crazy decision…. *(starts to go)* And Jack dear?

JACK. Yes, Momma.

MOMMA. No friends over when you're grounded.

MINSTREL. Oh…Sorry.

*(**MINSTREL** and **MOMMA** exit.)*

MINSTREL. *(poking his head back in)* Psst… Jack, guess you're on your own for this next part.

*(Now **JACK** is alone. He looks at his beans.)*

JACK. "Magic beans." Yeah. You're magic alright. You made all my stuff disappear! Well, now it's your turn. You're going to disappear. Right down the toilet!

*(The shadow light goes on. There's a big toilet shadow. **JACK** goes to the screen and mimes throwing beans into the bowl. Shadow beans fly out of his hand and land in the toilet bowl.)*

ACTORS BEHIND SCREEN. Sploosh! Splooshy!

JACK. And I won't be needing you either, will I?

*(**JACK** grabs the fertilizer bag and goes to the screen. He mimes dumping out the contents of the bag. Shadow dirt falls out of the bag into the toilet bowl. **JACK** flushes the toilet.)*

ACTORS BEHIND SCREEN. Splooshy sploosh…FLUSSHHH!

JACK. *(to the audience)* And I dusted off my hands. Nodded my head, and said "That is that."

*(Lights out – special on **JACK**.)*

JACK. But that wasn't that. That wasn't that at all.

Scene Six: The Beanstalk

(Shadow puppet screen: The beanstalk grows, twisting, getting longer, wider and leafier throughout the following.)

SONG: THINGS YOU THROW AWAY

MINSTREL. *(slowly, like a lullaby)*
THINGS YOU THROW AWAY
HAVE A FUNNY WAY
OF COMING BACK TO YOU
AND THINGS YOU THOUGHT THAT YOU HAD TRASHED
HAS A WAY OF COMING BACK
LIKE EVERYTHING YOU DO

EVERYTHING YOU DO OR SAY
HAS A FUNNY, FUNNY WAY
OF COMING BACK TO YOU
AND HAS A WAY OF KEEPING ON
GETTING BIGGER, GROWING STRONG
AFTER YOU ARE THROUGH
YES, AFTER YOU ARE THROUGH

(Lights fade out on the pretty music, Then – lights up with a screeching alarm clock sound.)

What the heck was that?

JACK. My alarm clock. I got up for school the next day. Tired. Still sleepy-eyed. Glad that the magic bean adventure was over. Went to the bathroom to wash-up and saw something sticking out of the toilet seat.

(A toilet has been placed Center Stage. **JACK** *lifts the lid and a giant beanstalk shoots straight up, knocking* **JACK** *to the floor and bursting through the ceiling! Debris falls from above.)*

JACK. Aaahh!… Oh, oh boy. Uhm, Momma?!

MOMMA. *(from off)* Jack? Are you alright? What's happened?

JACK. Uhm, it's the toilet, Momma. There's something… in it!

MOMMA. *(from off)* Jiggle the handle, sweetheart. It'll go down!

JACK. I don't think that's gonna work.

(**MOMMA** *enters.*)

MOMMA. If I have to get the plunger out – aahh!!! Jack, what have been eating?

JACK. It's the soybeans.

MOMMA. Well! I heard soy could make you gassy, but –

JACK. From the magic soybeans, Momma. I threw them out last night, flushed them down the toilet.

MOMMA. I'll call the plumber, *(looking up)* and the roofer. Oh my. We can't afford to fix all this.

JACK. How high do you think it goes? I can't even see the top.

MOMMA. Well, you're not going to find out. That soybean stalk is off limits, mister. Until you can figure a way to pay for this mess, you're still grounded. No, you're double grounded – double-double grounded – That's a quadruple grounding and – Jack, do you hear what I'm saying?

MINSTREL. That's when Jack heard a sound –

JACK. What's that sound?

MINSTREL. A sound that changed everything.

MOMMA. Where's it coming from?

MINSTREL. And it was coming from somewhere…

JACK. Up there.

MINSTREL. Wherever "up there" was – he heard it. It was a cry for help.

VOICE. Help! Help!

MOMMA. Jack, get to climbing. Here's your helmet. Up you go.

JACK. But you just said I was grounded. Double-triple grounded!

VOICE. Help!

MOMMA. Jackaroo, when a person is in trouble, do you focus on your own problems?

JACK. No, Momma.

MOMMA. That's right,

JACK & MOMMA. We try to help out.

MOMMA. It's the only way we get through in these hard times. Now hurry up, it sounds serious. But listen, Jack. Be careful. I'll be waiting for you.

(**JACK** *goes to climb the Beanstalk. Lights out.*)

(*Shadow Puppet Show: the leafy beanstalk goes from the roof of the house, at the bottom of the screen, all the way to the top of the screen. The little Jack puppet climbs out on the roof and grabs hold of the beanstalk. He climbs and climbs, sometimes losing his footing, but eventually he makes it to the top and disappears above the clouds.*)

Scene Seven: The Job above the Clouds

(Lights up – above the clouds.)

*(***JACK***, covered in vines/leaves, emerges from below the screen.)*

*(***MRS. BIG*** enters in a fluster.)*

MRS. BIG. Help! Help! Where is the help!?

JACK. What's wrong? What's wrong?

SONG: FINGERS TO THE BONE

MRS. BIG. My husband! He's going to be up soon and getting ready for work! The servants are missing. There's no breakfast, no newspaper, and most importantly – his shoes have not been shined! How can he go to work with his shoes not shined!?

MY HUSBAND HAS A GIANT OCCUPATION
HE IS THE BOSS OF MANY, MANY JOBS
OF COURSE HE GETS GIANT REMUNERATION
(THAT MEANS HE GETS PAID A LOT)
THAT'S GREAT FOR HIM BUT I'VE STILL GOT TO

WORK WORK WORK
MY FINGERS TO THE BONE
I WORK WORK WORK
ALL DAY AND ALL ALONE
I MAKE HIS GIANT MEALS AND I SCRUB HIS GIANT THRONE
I WORK, WORK, WORK, WORK MY FINGERS TO THE BONE.

(Music continues.)

JACK. What happened to the servants?

MRS. BIG. As usual – my husband has canned them.

JACK. Oh no! Your servants have lost their jobs?

MRS. BIG. If their jobs are to be boiled alive, mashed to a jelly, and sealed into a tin can, then they are gainfully employed.

MY HUSBAND HAS NO PATIENCE FOR MISTAKES
THOUGH EVERYONE CAN MAKE ONE NOW AND THEN

MRS. BIG. *(cont.)*

> YESTERDAY OUR COOK WAS
> BROILING A STEAK
> SHE FORGOT THE SPICE, SHE APOLOGIZED,
> BUT HE CHOPPED HER UP AND MADE COOK FRENCH FRIES
> CHOP CHOP! – SIZZLE SIZZLE!
> A PLUS SIZED WOMAN TO HIM IS LITTLE!
> I WORK WORK WORK
> MY FINGERS TO THE BONE
> I WORK WORK WORK
> TO KEEP HIS GIANT HOME
> TIME PASSES HERE LIKE A GIANT KIDNEY STONE
> I WORK, WORK, WORK, WORK MY FINGERS TO THE BONE

> Say, do you need a job?

> *(Music continues.)*

JACK. Me? I'm just a kid.

MRS. BIG. That's the spirit! You're never too young for your first job. *(places an apron on him)* Or your second. *(hands him polish and rag)* Or your third. *(hands him a giant clothespin)*

> MY HUSBAND IS A GIANT WORK-A-HOLIC
> HIS EYES ARE ALWAYS ON THE BOTTOM LINE
> NOW HE'S GOT THIS
> SECRET GOLDEN PROJECT
> THAT SUPPOSEDLY WILL CHANGE OUR LIVES
> YET SOMEHOW I SUSPECT THAT I'LL STILL

> WORK WORK WORK
> MY FINGERS TO THE BONE

JACK.

> WE'LL WORK WORK WORK
> CUZ NOW YOU'RE NOT ALONE

JACK & MRS. BIG.

> A CHORE CAN BE A PLEASURE
> IF YOU'RE NOT ALL ON YOUR OWN
> SO WE WORK WORK – WORK – WORK

> *(alternating now)*

> WORK – WORK – WORK – WORK

JACK & MRS. BIG. *(cont.) (together)*
WORK – WORK – WORK – OUR
FINGERS TO THE BONE!

JACK. Or we could just wear a good set of work gloves. *(awkward pause as Jack thinks this is very funny, but* **MRS. BIG** *does not)* What's all this stuff for?

MRS. BIG. The apron is for cooking and cleaning. The rag and polish are to shine my dear husband's beautiful giant shoes, and –

JACK. And the clothespin is for the laundry.

MRS. BIG. The clothespin is for your nose. Mr. Big has terrible foot odor. Come now! We must hurry before Mr. Big is late for work! Let's go let's go let's go!

(She hurries him off.)

Scene Eight: In the Giant's Kitchen

(Lights up in the kitchen of the Giant's mansion.)

*(**MRS. BIG** and **JACK** enter.)*

MRS. BIG. And this is the kitchen. You'll stay in here mostly. There's the sink, the stove, and here… *(She gestures to a giant shoe offstage.)* Here is one of my dear husband's shoes. You'll shine the left one today and tomorrow you can shine the right one.

*(**JACK** looks from the shoe to the can of polish in his hand and back again.)*

JACK. Gonna need more polish.

MRS. BIG. I want to see my face in that shoe.

JACK. You could see your whole body in that shoe… *(pointing to a large, covered object)* What's under there?

MRS. BIG. That's the super secret Golden Project Mr. Big has been working on. He says it will be our nest egg and we'll retire as trillionares. Listen now, this is most important. Stay out of sight. Do not let my husband see you here. When you hear him coming, hide until he leaves for his giant office and then you can come back out and finish your little jobs. Is that clear?

JACK. Clear as a bell.

MRS. BIG. I'll be back in a few hours. Now I must hurry over to the giant Swall-mart and pick-up as many unnecessary items as possible.

JACK. Why?

MRS. BIG. Excuse me?

JACK. Why are you buying things if you know you don't need them?

MRS. BIG. Because they're on sale! Oh! I almost forgot. I need you also to polish my husband's giant nametag.

(She produces a giant nametag that reads: "Mr. Big, President BARF inc.")

JACK. Mr. Big, president of "Barf?"

MRS. BIG. (*poking the nametag*) Big. Aggie. Reaping. Farms. Inc. – Remember – stay out of sight if you want to stay off my husband's giant dinner plate.

(*She exits.*)

JACK. "Big, Aggie, Reaping, Farms?" Now why does that name sound familiar?…Wow, this place is a palace. Mrs. Big said her husband is the Big Boss at this Big Aggie place. So, I bet that I can make these shoes shine soo bright – when he sees them he'll give me a giant bonus!

(*Music starts – hiphop music. Enter the golden **I-HARP**. The Golden **I-HARP** looks like an i-Pod, but with a picture of a classical harp on his giant screen. He wears a gold chain, big gold sunglasses and gold baseball cap. His earphones are plugged into the bottom of his costume.*)

(**JACK** *hides.*)

JACK. What the – wow! A golden i-…harp??

I-HARP. Good migady mornin', Mr. Big, Mr. Big. The only man who gets up in the mornin' just so he can lay it down! I know you like some music while you eat breakfast and you're gonna need your strength today! So, what's on the menu?

(*The ground shakes!! A pair of giant feet enter. The **GIANT***'s feet are all we see because he's sooo big!*)

GIANT. You're not paid to talk, i-Harp.

I-HARP. Too True. Too True. Talking's not my strong suit, but can I keep the beat like a crisper keeps carrots… Fresh!

SONG: THE GOLDEN GOOSE

MR. BIG.
FEE TO THE FI TO THE FO TO THE FUM
SERVANTS IN MY TUMMY MAKE ME SAY YUM-YUM
I CHEW THEM UP LIKE STICKS OF GUM
FEE TO THE FI TO THE FO TO THE FUM

I-HARP. Yeahhhhhh –

TODAY IS THE DAY
EVERYONE IS GONNA PAY
ALL THE DOLLARS AND DINEROS GONNA COME HIS WAY
MORE DOUGH, BIGGER CHEDDAR, GETTIN' CLAMS & BUCKS
WHEN THE PEOPLE GET A GANDER AT HIS GOLDEN DUCK.

(They uncover the "super secret golden project." It's the **GOOSE** *that lays the Golden Eggs. The Goose 'HONKS' and looks about.)*

MR. BIG. WHEN THE PEOPLE GET A GANDER AT MY GOLDEN DUCK!

JACK. That's not a duck, that's a goose.

(Sound of a record scratching – music stops. **JACK** *hides.)*

MR. BIG. Huh? Who's there?

I-HARP. Hey…Duck, goose – what's the difference, right? As long as she keeps laying you these giant golden eggs!

(The **GIANT** *laughs. Music continues.)*

I-HARP. Yeahhhhh

TODAY IS THE DAY
EVERYONE IS GONNA SAY
BIG AGGIE IS THE BIGGEST IN THE U.S.A.
DON'T STOP INTERNATIONAL IN EVERY LAND
HE'S THE MAN,

GIANT. I'm the man.

I-HARP.

CUZ IN HIS HANDS

GIANT/I-HARP.

I hold the golden goose!
    HE HOLDS THE GOLDEN GOOSE!
I hold the golden goose!
    HE HOLDS THE GOLDEN GOOSE!

EVERYDAY, ONCE A DAY
HE TELLS THIS GOOSE TO SIT AND LAY

MR. BIG. SIT! *(The* **GOOSE** *sits.)*

 LAY! *(The* **GOOSE** *lays a golden egg.)*

 And now I have a golden egg! AH-HAHAHAhahaha!
 When people get a gander at my goose's Golden Eggs,
 we'll put every farm on the planet out of business.
 We'll be the most powerful company in the whole wide
 world!

I-HARP. Yeahhhhhh….

 BUT ONE GOOD EGG BUT ONLY ONCE A DAY
 WILL NEVER FILL YOUR BELLY AS WELL AS, SAY,
 TWO – OR THREE – OR FOUR – OR FIVE –
 YOU'RE A GIANT! ONE-A-DAY CAN NEVER SATISFY

MR. BIG.

 MAYBE IF I MAKE HER EAT
 TENS TIMES MORE THAN A GOOSE SHOULD EAT
 OR MAYBE, MAYBE I SHOULD GIVE HER SHOTS

I-HARP. Yeah

 CHEMICALS TO MAKE HER LAY YOU LOTS AND LOTS

MR. BIG.

 INSIDE THE BELLY OF THIS GOLDEN GOOSE
 ARE ALL THE GOLDEN EGGS THAT I CAN USE
 WHY SHOULD I WAIT FOR NATURE TO TAKE ITS COURSE?
 I'LL GUT THIS GOOSE & GET THEM ALL BY FORCE!

GIANT/I-HARP.

 I hold the golden goose!

  HE HOLDS THE GOLDEN GOOSE!

 I hold the golden goose!

  HE HOLDS THE GOLDEN GOOSE!

 (Music vamps softly.)

MR. BIG. Yes, we'll make a little trip to the butcher shop,
 and my butcher will do the messy job of getting the
 eggs out of this goose! You, put this goose into her
 cage while I get ready for work.

 (Exit **MR. BIG.***)*

I-HARP. Lickety-splickety, Mr. Big…. Come on, Goose.
 Get in there. See, I know why the caged bird sings…
 Because it can't rap.

(Song ends.)

JACK. *(aside)* If I don't do something, that goose is a goner. But if I do go out there, it could be me that's on the dinner the plate.

MINSTREL. Jack found himself in a quandary; a pickle, a precarious predicament.

JACK. A what?

MINSTREL. A tough situation. He wiped his brow and he thought:

JACK.	MINSTREL.
I wish I'd never heard of these stupid magic beans.	I wish I'd never heard of these stupid magic beans. Heard of – Heard of.

JACK. Never *heard*, eh? …Hmm.

MINSTREL. Just then…

JACK. Gives me an idea.

MINSTREL. Jack got an idea…ssshh.

I-HARP. *(to the* GOOSE*)* Come on, Goosey, you don't have to rage against the machine. I keep your cage nice and –

*(*JACK *sneaks up behind the* I-HARP *and unplugs the* I-HARP*'s earphone plug.)*

(The I-HARP *turns to yell for help, but he can't make a sound! He yells and yells but no sound comes out. He runs off, waving frantically.)*

JACK. Now with that loud mouth out of the way – we'll make a sneaky retreat. I took the goose in my arms, and tip-toed right out the –

(The GIANT *enters, blocking* JACK*'s way.* JACK*, sneaking out, backs into the Giant Foot. He leaps.)*

JACK. OH! Uhm. Hello, uhm, Mr. Big. I'm uhm. I'm your new servant.

MR. BIG. Oh? And just what are you doing with that goose?

JACK. Uhm…polishing. Yeah. Polishing your shoes! See?

MR. BIG. What's your name, servant?

JACK. My name? Uhm…my name is Jack.

MR. BIG. Jack, you say? That's a good name.

JACK. Oh yeah?

MR. BIG. A delicious name. I love Cracker Jacks.

JACK. Uh-oh.

MR. BIG. And I very much enjoy Monterey Jack cheese.

JACK. Oh-boy.

MR. BIG. But my favorite dish of all is freshly… canned… servant.

JACK. Gulp.

(**MR. BIG** *kicks* **JACK**, *and* **JACK** *falls down on his knees.*)

MR. BIG. You're not a servant! You're trying to steal my goose, and that makes you a fowl crook!

GOOSE. Hoooonk!

MR. BIG. Give me the goose, Jack. If I don't get those eggs then I'm out of a job.

JACK. But wait! If you hurt this goose – then you're still out of a job! Don't you see? You can get a lot of eggs all at once, sure, but then – that's it. No more eggs – Ever! But – If you conserve, you know – take just one egg at a time like it was meant to be, then she can lay you golden eggs for years and years and years!

GOOSE. Honk-Honk-Honk!

MR. BIG. Who cares about years and years?! I'm here today, and I want it all now!

JACK. Well what about your kids then!? What about all the kids? Like me!

MINSTREL. Like us!

JACK. Yeah! Like them! Don't you think they deserve to have Golden Eggs in the future?

MR. BIG. Big Aggie Reaping Farms doesn't care about your cute little friends – or their cute little futures. This is a business, and the company only cares about one thing: the bottom line!

JACK. The bottom line? What's that?

MR. BIG. The bottom line is how much money we make at the end of this one day. And your day is about to end right now, Jack!

(**MR. BIG**'s *foot rises to squish* **JACK**.)

(**JACK** *pulls out his big clothespin in the nick of time, and pinches it on* **MR. BIG**'s *big toe.*)

MR. BIG. Yow!!!

JACK. I hate to egg you on, Mr. Big, but this seems like a golden opportunity!

MR. BIG. Come back with my goose, you turkey! You can't stand in the way of big business!!

JACK. That's why I'm getting as far out of the way as possible! *(exiting – aside)* Why do I suspect this is going to turn into a wild goose chase?

MR. BIG. Your goose is cooked, Jack! You'll never work on this cloud again!

(**JACK** *runs off.* **MR. BIG** *chases.*)

(*Music from "BLOWN AROUND" – lights out – Music continues into…*)

(*Shadow Puppet Show: Little puppet Jack is running from Mr. Big the Giant. He runs and runs, narrowly escaping being squished to a pancake. He dives for the tip of the beanstalk that's sticking out of the cloud below him.*)

Scene Nine: Escaping the Giant

(**JACK**'s *bedroom.* **MOM** *is in climbing gear, and she's about to go up the beanstalk.*)

MOMMA.
JACK, I FEEL THAT SOMETHING'S WRONG
I FEAR YOU'VE MET DISASTER
I'M YOU'RE MOTHER. IT'S MY JOB.
NOW I'M CLIMBING AFTER.

(*A soybean pod and some leaves fall from above and hit her on the helmet.* **JACK** *enters.*)

MOMMA. What the?! Jack!?

JACK. Get the axe!

MOMMA. Huh?

JACK. Dad's axe! Get dad's axe! He's right behind me! HURRY!!

MOMMA. Where am I going to find an Axe?! (*It's handed to her from behind the shadow screen.*) Ah, Axe!

(*A* **GIANT FOOT** *appears above.*)

MOMMA. Is that a foot?!

JACK. That's Mr. Big, the big-big boss. He's trying to can me!

MOMMA. You got a job? Honey, I'm so proud!

(**JACK** *trades his mother the goose for the axe. He raises the axe to swing.*)

JACK. Watch out, Mom!…Hey goose, duck.
(*He swings the axe. A cracking sound. The beanstalk sways.*)
(*The* **GIANT FOOT** *kicks wildly.*)
(*Black out with strobe – The beanstalk sways this way – then it sways that way. The earth rumbles beneath their feet. There's an explosion!! Music stops.*)
(*Lights up. The place is a wreck.* **MOMMA** *and* **JACK** *have smoky smears on their faces.* **JACK** *picks up the* **GOLDEN GOOSE.**)

MOM. Oh my, Jack. That was close.

JACK. Totally. Mr. Big tried to can me, but in the end I gave him the axe. *(holding up the axe)*

MOMMA. What happened up there?

MINSTREL. *(to us)* So Jack told his mom about everything that had happened since he went up the beanstalk. And he told her what Mr. Big said about the corporation only caring about "the bottom line,"…and she said:

MOMMA. A company isn't a person, Jack. It's just a thing. Only a person can care about another person.

*(**MOMMA** hugs **JACK** tightly.)*

Oh, Jack! I'm just so glad you're back home to me and safe. If I lost you, all the money in the world wouldn't be worth a pile of beans.

JACK. Awww, Mom!

MOMMA. The roof is completely ruined though. How are we going to fix that?

*(**MINSTREL** clears his throat – points to the **GOOSE** in **JACK**'s hands.)*

JACK. Oh yeah. Tomorrow, our new friend here will lay us a golden egg. Then we'll buy a new roof. And I think we should invest in a solar paneled, wind powered, hydro-electric roof that will heat and cool our home with the rays of the sun, the scent of honeysuckle on the breeze and the feeling of change in the air.

MOMMA. Jack, honey, I don't think that kind of roof exists.

JACK. Well, not with that attitude it doesn't.

SONG: YOU DON'T KNOW JACK (REPRISE)

MINSTREL.

SO THERE THE STORY WENT
I'D SAY THAT'S TIME WELL SPENT
WE LAUGHED, WE CRIED, IT'S ALMOST FADE-TO-BLACK.
WE FACED DOWN DISASTER
AND NOW IT'S HAPPY EVER AFTER
NOW WE KNOW THE STORY, AND THAT'S ALMOST A WRAP

SO SURELY WE CAN SAY ———
SAY WE KNOW JACK.

SONG: THINGS YOU THROW AWAY (REPRISE)

(All the characters revert back to their actor-selves like when we first met them in scene one, but they are noted here as the characters they played.)

JACK.

LIFE IS LIKE A GARDEN
ONE YOU PUT YOUR HEART IN.
ROWS AND ROWS OF FERTILE SOIL READY FOR THE SEEDS.

MOMMA.

BE MINDFUL OF THE CROPS YOU SOW
SOMETIMES IN LIFE IT'S HARD TO KNOW
THE FLOWERS FROM THE WEEDS.

*(***FARMER*** enters.)*

FARMER.

THROW GARBAGE IN YOUR GARDEN
SPILL OIL, DRIVE A CAR IN,
AND NOTHING GOOD WILL GROW
Don't ya know?

MOM & FARMER.

BUT IF YOU WATER IT WITH CARE
TILL THE SOIL, CLEAN THE AIR,
YOU'LL SEE THE GOODNESS FLOW

MRS. BIG.

AND WHEN YOU HELP A NEIGHBOR
WHO NEEDS A LITTLE BOOST
THAT'S A SEED YOU'VE PLANTED THAT WILL GROW THE
    SWEETEST FRUITS.

SECURITY GUARD.

SO LET'S PLANT THEM DEEP IN THE EARTH

SECURITY & I-HARP.

IT'S NOT TO LATE FOR A RE-BEARTH
IF WE CAN CHANGE OUR TUNE

ALL.

CUZ EVERYTHING YOU DO OR SAY
HAS A FUNNY, FUNNY WAY OF COMING BACK TO YOU
AND THINGS YOU THINK THAT YOU CAN TRASH

DON'T GO AWAY, THEY COME RIGHT BACK
LIKE EVERYTHING YOU DO

YES EVERYTHING YOU DO OR SAY
HAS THAT FUNNY FUNNY WAY
OF COMING BACK TO YOU
AND HAS A WAY OF KEEPING ON
GETTING BIGGER GROWING STRONG
AFTER YOU ARE THROUGH,
AND NOW OUR STORY'S THROUGH ———

(curtain)

PROPERTIES

Video game controller
Toilet with a beanstalk that grows out of it
Pick-up truck with a wind-sail made out of a cardboard box
Giant B.A.R.F. Inc. name tag
Beanstalk leaves
Bag of beans
A golden egg
An axe/hatchet
Bag of fertelizer
Gardening gloves
Apron
Rag
Over-sized clothespin
Box for goose to sit in
Fabric to cover goose

A NOTE ON THE SOYBEAN PUPPETS

To create the Soybean Muppet-style hand puppets that danced and sang in the original production of the song "THE MAGIC BEAN" one only needs some typical cushion foam, cloth fabric, cardboard, spray glue, needle, thread, and an electric knife. There are many books and websites that will show you all sorts of ways to make terrific looking hand puppets. The ingredients listed here should not be used without adult supervision.

www.ingramcontent.com/pod-product-compliance
Lightning Source LLC
Chambersburg PA
CBHW070403120726
47909CB00008B/2974